Neptune's Ghost
and other scary stories

Neptune's Ghost
and other scary stories

Written by
Caroline Repchuk, Geoff Cowan
and Claire Keen

Illustrated by
Robin Edmonds, Chris Forsey
and Diana Catchpole

p

This is a Parragon book
First published in 2000

Parragon
Queen Street House
4 Queen Street
Bath BA1 1HE, UK

Produced by
The Templar Company plc,
Pippbrook Mill, London Road,
Dorking, Surrey RH4 1JE UK

Edited by Caroline Repchuk

Designed by Caroline Reeves

Printed and bound in Spain
ISBN 0 75253 407 6

Contents

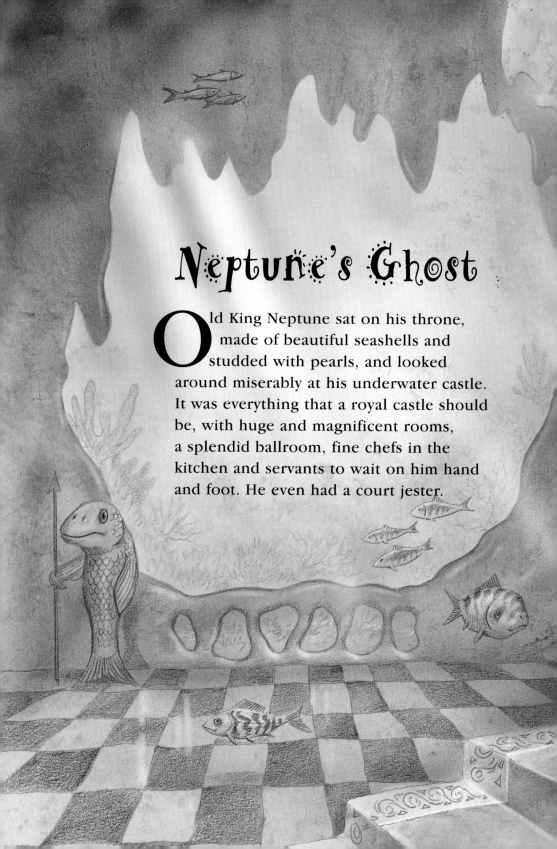

Neptune's Ghost

Old King Neptune sat on his throne, made of beautiful seashells and studded with pearls, and looked around miserably at his underwater castle. It was everything that a royal castle should be, with huge and magnificent rooms, a splendid ballroom, fine chefs in the kitchen and servants to wait on him hand and foot. He even had a court jester.

But there was one thing missing — the castle had no ghost, and as everyone knows, all proper castles should be haunted! And the fact that his castle had no ghost was getting poor old King Neptune down. So he sat on his throne frowning, as he tried to think what to do.

Just then, the little court jester appeared. He was a young octopus called Oscar, who had delighted the king with his juggling tricks when he applied for the job. He was also very good at telling jokes, and he tried one out on the king now, to see if he could cheer him up:

"Excuse me, your Majesty, but what do you get if you cross a newspaper with a sleeping pill?" he asked, cheekily. "...A snoozepaper!"

The king, who had been staring absent-mindedly into space, suddenly looked startled, then let out a loud guffaw!

"Brilliant! Oscar you are brilliant! Why ever didn't I think of it before?"

"It wasn't that good a joke, your Majesty," said the little jester, rather bewildered.

"Never mind jokes right now," said the king. "Fetch me a pen and a piece of paper."

The king took up the pen and in no time at all he had drafted out an advertisement:

'Wanted: One ghost for royal castle. Must be good at haunting, making spooky noises, and walking through walls. Excellent rates of pay, two weeks holiday, and free luncheon vouchers for successful applicant. Apply at King Neptune's castle.'

"Here," said the king, handing the piece of paper to Oscar. "Put this advertisement in the *Ocean Times*. We should have a ghost in the castle in no time!" And he sat back in his throne and smiled to himself in satisfaction.

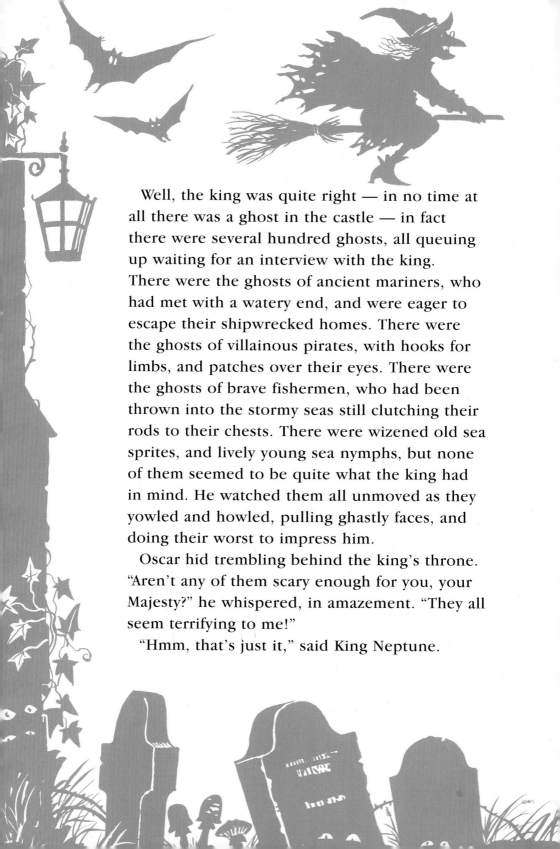

Well, the king was quite right — in no time at all there was a ghost in the castle — in fact there were several hundred ghosts, all queuing up waiting for an interview with the king. There were the ghosts of ancient mariners, who had met with a watery end, and were eager to escape their shipwrecked homes. There were the ghosts of villainous pirates, with hooks for limbs, and patches over their eyes. There were the ghosts of brave fishermen, who had been thrown into the stormy seas still clutching their rods to their chests. There were wizened old sea sprites, and lively young sea nymphs, but none of them seemed to be quite what the king had in mind. He watched them all unmoved as they yowled and howled, pulling ghastly faces, and doing their worst to impress him.

Oscar hid trembling behind the king's throne. "Aren't any of them scary enough for you, your Majesty?" he whispered, in amazement. "They all seem terrifying to me!"

"Hmm, that's just it," said King Neptune.

"They're all far too scary. Too big, and rough, and ugly. What I really wanted was a little ghost like the one in my storybook." He pulled out a large book from under his throne, and pointed to a picture of a fluffy little white ghost peeking out from behind a fairytale king's throne.

Just then, a haunting little sound echoed in his ears. The king shivered. "What was that?" he asked. But before Oscar could reply, the sound came again, and a fuzzy little white shape came floating through the wall. There before the king hovered the ghost of a little white whale, who had perished when he got caught in some fishing nets, and had been roaming the oceans of the world looking for a home ever since.

The king blinked, and rubbed his eyes.
"Perfect!" he cried and, dismissing all the other
applicants, he offered the ghostly little whale
the job on the spot. The little whale accepted
happily, and the king smiled with satisfaction.

Now his castle had everything that a proper
royal castle should have. And so this tale has
the ending that every proper fairytale should
have — that they all lived happily ever after!

Phantom Footsteps

Phantom footsteps in the hallway,
The heavy door creaks open wide,
A creepy voice speaks out of nowhere:
"Step this way, do come inside."

Candles flicker in the darkness,
A floating lantern leads the way,
Down silent hall and empty passage,
Cold draughts blow and shadows play.

Cobwebs stretch from every corner,
Overhead hang sleeping bats,
Portraits watch as you creep by them,
On the floor run squeaking rats!

The lantern leads into the great hall,
Dimly lit by candlelight,
Empty, but for one large coffin —
What a dreaded, fearful sight!

As you approach the lid creaks open,
A ghostly figure smiles at you,
Holds out a hand, and bids you welcome —
"Have some tea, one lump or two?"

It's good to make friends with your neighbours,
For who knows what could be in store,
So don't refuse an invitation,
If a *vampire* moves next door!

Stand and Deliver

It was a dark and stormy night. Thunder crashed, rain lashed, lightning flashed and, jolting along inside the royal horse and carriage, poor King Penniless felt bruised and bashed!

He had been away on important business, trying unsuccessfully to raise funds to help save his crumbling castle from falling apart. For although he was a king, he was not a wealthy one, having lost all his money in a series of bad investments. He was a kind and gentle king, but he had no head for business. King Penniless leaned back inside his carriage and closed his eyes. What could he do to save himself from ruin?

The royal horse and carriage battled on along the bumpy road that crossed the wild and windy moor. The glass rattled in the carriage windows, and a steady stream of water poured in through a leak in the roof, and dripped onto the king's head.

"What a sorry state to be in," the king thought, miserably. Just then, with a loud whinny, the horses reared up in fright,

and the carriage came crashing to a halt.

"Stand and deliver!" boomed an eerie voice outside. King Penniless nervously lowered the window and peered out into the stormy night, but it was so dark that he couldn't see anything at all. "What's the matter?" the king called to his coachman, trying to sound braver than he felt.

"It.. it's the Gh-ghostly Highwayman!" stuttered his terrified coachman in reply.

"Ghosts, bish-bosh!" called King Penniless, crossly. "It's just the wind. Drive on!"

"I c-can't sir," replied the coachman. "We've lost a wheel."

"Well, hurry up and replace it!" ordered the king. This was all he needed! He was tired and worn out with worry, and he just wanted to get home, put his feet up and have a nice hot cup of cocoa.

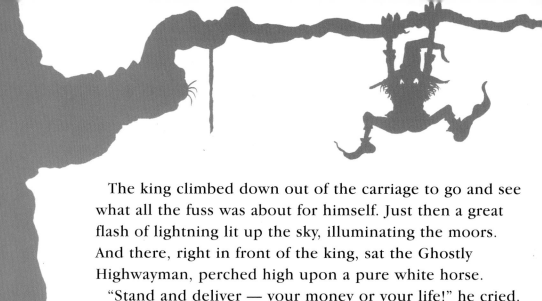

The king climbed down out of the carriage to go and see what all the fuss was about for himself. Just then a great flash of lightning lit up the sky, illuminating the moors. And there, right in front of the king, sat the Ghostly Highwayman, perched high upon a pure white horse.

"Stand and deliver — your money or your life!" he cried. His cape swirled around his ashen face, as he pointed an old-fashioned pistol at the king.

Well, the poor king trembled so hard that his teeth started to chatter.

"B..but I d..don't have any money!" he stuttered.

"Nonsense!" cried the Highwayman. "You're the king aren't you?"

"Y-yes — but I'm nearly bankrupt," said the king, and as it seemed there was nothing else for it, he went on to explain his position to his ghostly listener.

By the time the king had finished telling him the story of all his troubles, the Ghostly Highwayman was almost in tears. "How terrible for you," he said. "But there must be some way I can help. Let's think of a plan!"

"Help!" spluttered the king. "Why would you want to help? A moment ago you were threatening to shoot me!"

"I'm sorry. I didn't mean it," said the Ghostly Highwayman. "It's just part of the act. That's what highwaymen are supposed to say. I only stopped your carriage because it's lonely out here, and I wanted someone to talk to."

"Well there are better ways of making friends than waving pistols at people!" said the king, indignantly.

"You're right," said the ghost. "It's just that being a highwayman is all I know, although I was never very good at it — I suppose that's why I got caught. And it was thanks to your great-grandfather that I escaped the gallows, so really I owe you a favour."

He went on to explain how the king's great-grandfather had granted him a royal pardon, after his daughter, the young Princess Angelina,

had pleaded for the highwayman's life to be spared, as they were secretly in love. But no amount of crying could persuade her father to let them marry, and so she hid away in a tower, dressed in grey, and died of a broken heart.

"The Lady in Grey!" cried the king.

"You've heard of her?" asked the Ghostly Highwayman, excitedly.

"Heard of her? I've *seen* her!" said the king. "She's still up there, weeping and wailing. It keeps us all awake at night — I haven't had a good night's sleep in years! No one goes near the tower for fear of her, though I did creep up and take a peek when I was a young lad."

"But this is wonderful!" cried the highwayman. "And it's given me an idea for a way to solve *all* our problems!.."

"Stand and deliver! Your money or your life!" boomed the Ghostly Highwayman. The two middle-aged ladies squealed with terror and delight, and quickly handed over their entrance fee for a place on the next tour of the haunted royal castle! The Lady in Grey smiled and winked at the highwayman as she stepped through the wall, let out a ghostly wail, and glided up the staircase. "Follow me!" she called. An eager bunch of tourists clambered up the stairs behind her, watched happily by the king, as he counted the day's takings.

"At this rate, the castle will be restored in no time!" said the king to the Ghostly Highwayman, rubbing his hands together in delight. "How can I ever thank you?"

"Being reunited with the Princess is reward enough," said the Ghostly Highwayman.

"Plus I don't have to live out on that windy moor any longer, holding people up just to have someone to talk to. There's only one thing more I could wish for — Princess Angelina's hand in marriage."

"Brilliant!" said the king. "A ghostly royal wedding. Now that should really bring in the crowds!.."

And as the king settled down to sleep that night, he gave a contented sigh. At last he could sleep in peace!

Take the Ghost Train

There's a tumbledown old station,
Where a ghost train waits to go.
All aboard, ghosts, ghouls and goblins,
Watch the engine brightly glow!

In its cab, a phantom fireman,
Helps the engine get up steam.
Chuff-chuff-chuff, it's moving slowly,
Hear its whistle, like a screeeeam!

Ghostly guards are whistling wildly,
Bony fingers wave goodbye,
As along the rails the ghost train glides,
Beneath the moonlit sky.

Witches shriek along the railcars,
While inside the dining car,
Vampires munch and crunch with monsters,
Sipping cocktails at the bar!

On they speed through misty marshes,
What a chilling sight to see.
Ghostly faces at the windows,
Silent wheels turn eerily!

If there were tickets for the ghost train,
Would you dare to take a ride?
Or would you quickly run away,
And find somewhere to hide!

All Done and Dusted

Duster was a witch's cat. He came
from a long line of witches' cats,
a fact of which he was very proud,
for he and his ancestors were known far
and wide to be very fine witches' cats
indeed. He lived in a little cottage with a
kind witch called Mavis, of whom he was
very fond. Mavis thanked her lucky stars
for Duster, and told him often that he was
the best cat a witch could wish for. So you
would think that Duster would be happy
and content, but he wasn't. You see, Duster
had a problem – and a rather mucky
problem at that.

Now, as you know, cats are clean and tidy creatures. They wash at least ten times a day, and are carefully groomed at all times. They are light on their feet and can tiptoe across crowded surfaces without making a sound or knocking anything over.

But witches are a completely different matter. They only wash twice a year (Christmas and birthdays). They crash about, knocking things over (like pots of sticky green slime), and they never wash anything up after using it. And of all the grimy, slimy, mucky, messy witches, Mavis was the worst. Only that morning Duster had used up another one of his nine lives when he slipped in a pool of snail slime on the floor, tripped over Mavis' broomstick, that as usual had been left lying on the floor, and was catapulted across the room, narrowly missing the bubbling cauldron on the fire. Poor Duster was at the end of his tether.

So it was with a heavy heart that he sat thinking how to celebrate his birthday, which was in a few days time. He wanted to have a few friends over, but the cottage was in such a mess that he felt too embarrassed. But while he was pondering what to do, Mavis suddenly announced that she had to go and visit her sister, Ethel for a few days.

Apparently, Ethel had cast a spell to turn everything she touched into chocolate, but as it was the middle of summer her whole cottage was melting into one big sticky mess.

"It's very kind of you to go and help Ethel tidy up," said Duster.

"Oh, I can't wait," said Mavis, loading her bags onto her broomstick. "Every witch in the forest will be there, it will be a real party."

"I don't understand," said Duster, watching Mavis from the safety of the window sill. "None of you are exactly good at housework."

"Housework!" Mavis spluttered. "Who said anything about *housework*? We're not going to *clean* her house — we're going to *eat* it!" she chuckled, licking her lips and patting her round belly. "We'll make chocolate custard, chocolate mousse, chocolate cake, chocolate chip cookies..." And still muttering about chocolate, she hopped on her broomstick and flew away.

Duster tutted in disapproval. The only time witches cleared anything up was when there was food involved, which is why all witches have very clean fridges.

As Duster tucked himself into bed that night an idea came to him. While Mavis was at her sister's, he could clean up the cottage and invite his friends over for a birthday tea. After all, many springs had come and gone without a clean — it was high time he took action!

The next morning, Duster got up bright and early, put on his apron and got straight to work. First of all he cleared everything into the garden so that he could see what he was doing. He swept the floor and polished it till it shone. Then he scrubbed the table and covered it with a nice clean tablecloth. Next, he dusted the bookshelves, being careful not to open the spellbooks in case any magic fell out.

He hadn't forgotten the time a rainbow spell leaked onto his tail — it kept changing colour for months, which he found very embarassing.

He sorted out the jars and bottles, putting spell ingredients on the dresser and food in the kitchen. Mavis was always getting her spells and recipes mixed up — you never knew what you might find in your soup!

Duster washed out the cauldron, which was splashed with all sorts of potions. When he wrang out his cloth, a slimy green puddle formed, turned into a toad, and hopped off.

Finally, Duster decorated the cottage with balloons and streamers and laid out a party tea with a birthday cake in the shape of a mouse.

He stood back and looked around, feeling very pleased with himself.

At two o'clock the door bell rang and as Duster let his friends in they marvelled at the lovely clean cottage.

"You two *have* been busy," said Sparkle. "However did you get Mavis to clear up?"

"I didn't. She's staying at her sister's, so I took the opportunity to tidy up myself," said Duster, and he went on to explain the plan he'd made. "As you all know, I come from a famous family of witches' cats, but being a witch's cat is not what it used to be. Standards have slipped, and I've had enough. I can't go on living in such a terrible mess. I'm going to tell Mavis that either she keeps the place tidy, or I'm going on strike! That should make her mend her ways. After all, no witch can do without her cat!"

"Good for you, that's the idea!" cheered the others.

"If only we could all do the same!" said Sweep.

"But we can!" cried Bristle. "All the witches have gone to Ethel's. We can *all* clean our cottages!" The cats all nodded excitedly, and happily discussed their cleaning plans while enjoying the birthday tea.

A few days later, Mavis came hurtling through the door on her broomstick, but she stopped in her tracks when she saw the cottage.

"Oh my, what have you done? Where are all my things? cried Mavis.

"It's all right, they're all here. I've just tidied them up," said Duster, opening cupboards and showing her. "There are going to be a few changes around here from now on," he went on firmly, and explained his ultimatum to Mavis. All over the forest the other cats were doing just the same.

After much grumbling and complaining, Mavis sulkily agreed to keep tidy. "But I still liked it better messy," she muttered.

"Too late!" said Duster. "It's all done and dusted! Now let's have a nice cup of tea." And from then on, Duster was a very happy witch's cat indeed.

Ode to Ghosts

A ghost he has a sad old life
Haunting empty castles.
On birthdays and at Christmas time
The postman brings no parcels.

He floats around from room to room,
He howls and clanks his chains.
But everyone ignores the noise,
And blames it on the drains.

And if by chance he should appear
Most people scream with fright.
He just can't understand it —
Is he *such* a dreadful sight?

He has no friends to play with
It really is a shame.
He'd like to come around for tea,
Or join you in a game.

But people think that ghosts are bad
And so they stay away.
There's no-one he can natter to,
Or pass the time of day.

So if you ever meet a ghost
Don't run away in fright.
Stay awhile and have a chat,
You'll find they're most polite.